For Karen, Judith and Gary,
who I have always been able
to 'count' on!

Red Robin Books is an imprint of Corner To Learn Limited

Published by
Corner To Learn Limited
Willow Cottage ● 26 Purton Stoke
Swindon ● Wiltshire SN5 4JF ● UK

ISBN: 978-1-905434-13-8

First published in the UK 2008
Text © Neil Griffiths 2008
Illustrations © Judith Blake 2008

Design by
David Rose

Printed by
Tien Wah Press Pte. Ltd., Singapore

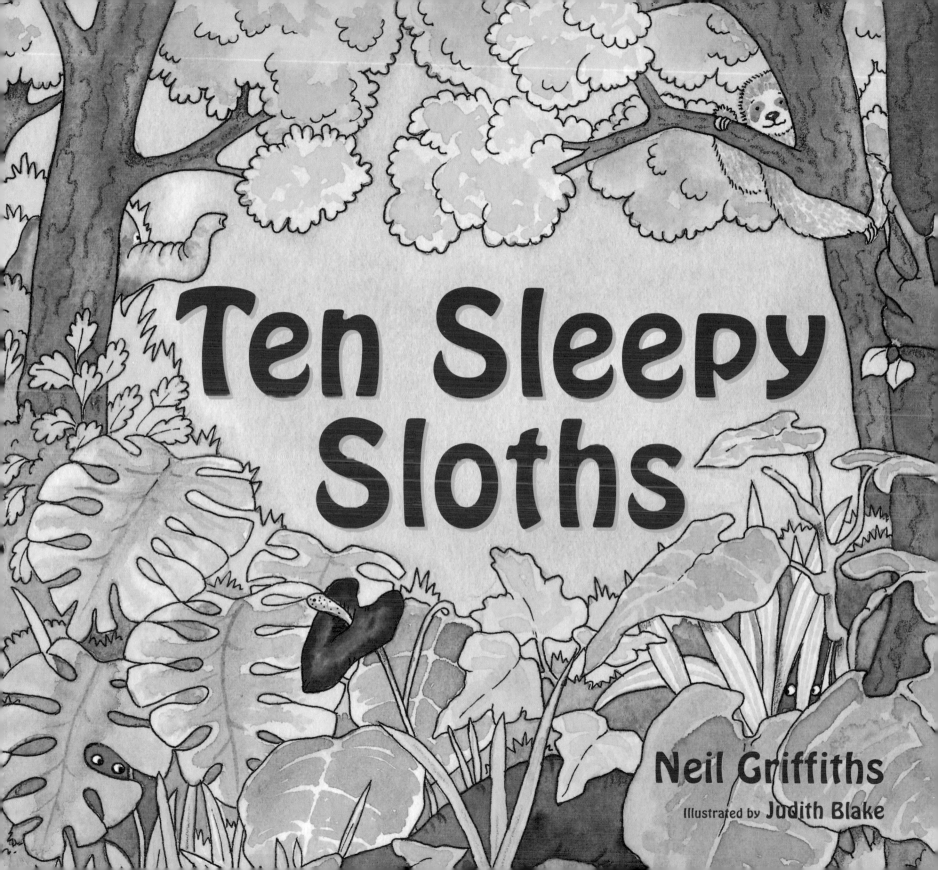

Ten Sleepy Sloths

Neil Griffiths

Illustrated by **Judith Blake**

Ten sleepy sloths hanging from a tree,
Ten sleepy sloths hanging from a tree,
And if two sleepy sloths slope slowly off for tea,
Then how many sloths left hanging in the tree?

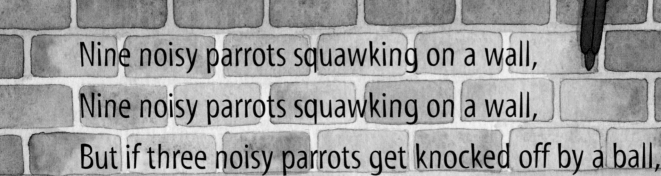

Nine noisy parrots squawking on a wall,
Nine noisy parrots squawking on a wall,
But if three noisy parrots get knocked off by a ball,
Then how many parrots left squawking on a wall?

Eight growling polars enjoy a lovely roll,

Eight growling polars enjoy a lovely roll,

And if two growling polars plod off to the North Pole,

Then how many polars left having a lovely roll?

Seven thirsty elephants have a nice cool sip,

Seven thirsty elephants have a nice cool sip,

And if three thirsty elephants dive in and have a dip,

Then how many elephants left trying to have a sip?

Six hungry penguins perching on a rock,
Six hungry penguins perching on a rock,
But if four hungry penguins get an unexpected shock,
Then how many penguins left perching on a rock?

Five furry fruit bats flying in the night,
Five furry fruit bats flying in the night,
And if two furry fruit bats give themselves a fright,
Then how many fruit bats left flying in the night?

Four hungry pandas, chew and chew and chew,
Four hungry pandas, chew and chew and chew,
But if two hungry pandas sneak off for more bamboo,
Then how many pandas left to chew and chew?

Three hefty hippos snoozing in the mud,
Three hefty hippos snoozing in the mud,
But if one hefty hippo goes glug and glug and glug,
Then how many hippos left snoozing in the mud?

Two timid zebras standing side by side,
Two timid zebras standing side by side,
But if one timid zebra decides to go and hide,
Then how many zebras left wishing they could hide?

One lazy lion dozing in the sun,

One lazy lion dozing in the sun,

But if one lazy lion decides to have some fun,

Then all you can see is 'absolutely none'!